DON'T DO THAT!

DON'T DO THAT!

by Tony Ross

Red Fox

A Red Fox Book

Published by Random House Children's Books, 20 Vauxhall Bridge Road, London SW1V 2SA

A division of Random House UK Ltd., London, Melbourne, Sydney, Auckland, Johannesburg and agencies throughout the world

First published by Andersen Press Limited 1991. Red Fox edition 1992. © Tony Ross 1991

Printed in Hong Kong

ISBN 0 09 991710 6

Nellie had a pretty nose.

It was so pretty that it won pretty nose competitions.

It was so pretty that Nellie was given a part in the Christmas play, with Donna and Patricia, who had pretty noses too.

"CHILDREN, don't do that!" said teacher.

"It won't come out, sir," said Nellie. "It's *stuck.*"

The teacher tried to get Nellie's finger out, but he couldn't.

Neither could the head teacher.
"It's stuck," they said, and sent Nellie home.

"It's stuck," said Nellie.
"I can get it out," said Henry.
"Mum," shouted Nellie.

But Mum couldn't get Nellie's finger out.
"I can," said Henry.

So Mum called the doctor.
"I can't get it out," he said.
"I can," said Henry.

So the doctor called the police.
"We can't get it out," they said.
"I can," said Henry.

So the police called the conjurer.
"I can't get it out," he said.
"I can," said Henry.

So the conjurer called the farmer.
"I can't get it out," said the farmer.
"I can," said Henry.

So the farmer called the fire brigade.
"We can't get it out," they said.
"I can," said Henry.

Nobody could get Nellie's finger out.
Her nose was longer, and it hurt.
There was only one thing left to do.

"I can get it out," said Henry.

So everybody called the scientist.
"Of course I can get it out," he said . . .

... "Science can do anything."
And he measured Nellie's nose.
"I can get it out," said Henry.

So the scientist built a rocket ship, and tied it to Nellie's arm.

Then he tied Nellie's leg to the park bench.

Then he set off the rocket,

...but Nellie's finger *still* wouldn't come out.

"I can get it out," said Henry.

"Go on then!" said the teachers, Mum, the doctor, the police, the conjurer, the farmer, the fire brigade and the scientist.

So Henry tickled Nellie . . .
. . . and it worked!

The
end →

Some bestselling Red Fox picture books

THE BIG ALFIE AND ANNIE ROSE STORYBOOK
by Shirley Hughes
OLD BEAR
by Jane Hissey
JOHN PATRICK NORMAN McHENNESSY –
THE BOY WHO WAS ALWAYS LATE
by John Burningham
I WANT A CAT
by Tony Ross
NOT NOW, BERNARD
by David McKee
THE STORY OF HORRIBLE HILDA AND HENRY
by Emma Chichester Clark
THE SAND HORSE
by Michael Foreman and Ann Turnbull
BAD BORIS GOES TO SCHOOL
by Susie Jenkin-Pearce
MRS PEPPERPOT AND THE BILBERRIES
by Alf Prøysen
BAD MOOD BEAR
by John Richardson
WHEN SHEEP CANNOT SLEEP
by Satoshi Kitamura
THE LAST DODO
by Ann and Reg Cartwright
IF AT FIRST YOU DO NOT SEE
by Ruth Brown
THE MONSTER BED
by Jeanne Willis and Susan Varley
DR XARGLE'S BOOK OF EARTHLETS
by Jeanne Willis and Tony Ross
JAKE
by Deborah King

H13